THE
LION KING

The sun rose high in the sky and beat down on the plains of Africa.

Through the shimmering heat came birds and animals of all shapes and sizes – from the smallest ant to the mightiest elephant. Giraffes, antelope, zebras – all were hurrying towards Pride Rock, to welcome Prince Simba, the newborn son of Mufasa, the Lion King, and Queen Sarabi.

A buzz of excitement ran through the crowd of animals gathered at the base of Pride Rock. Rafiki, a mystic, old baboon, began the slow steep climb to the top.

Above his head fluttered a blue-feathered hornbill. The bird, who was the King's adviser, circled twice above the crowd, then flew straight to the summit. He landed at the feet of a magnificent lion. "King Mufasa," reported the hornbill to his master, "everyone is here."

The King nodded. "Thank you, Zazu," he replied.

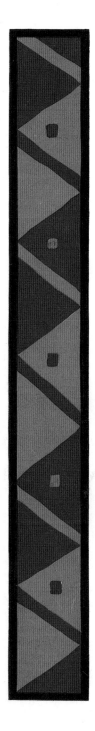

At last Rafiki's long climb came to an end. Silence fell as the baboon approached Queen Sarabi and the sleepy cub, nestling comfortably between her paws.

Rafiki smiled. "He looks exactly like you did when you were a cub," he told Mufasa. The little cub opened his eyes and yawned. Rafiki blessed the new Prince, then gently carried him to the edge of Pride Rock.

As Rafiki held the tiny cub high above his head, the animals below shouted and cheered, "Welcome! Welcome Prince Simba, our future king!"

*   *   *

But not everyone was pleased with the arrival of the little Prince. Scar, the King's brother, was jealous of Simba, for he wanted to become king himself.

After Simba had been blessed, King Mufasa went in search of Scar to ask why he had missed the ceremony. But Scar refused to answer and stalked away, twitching his tail angrily.

The days passed quickly for Simba, who was a happy, lively cub. One morning he woke very early and trotted off to find his father, who was fast asleep next to Sarabi. Leaping onto the King's back, Simba first whispered and then called *very* loudly, "Hey Father! Wake up!"

The King stirred and grumbled to Sarabi as he slowly woke up. Once he was awake, he led Simba on a long walk through the vast Pride Lands.

"Look, Simba," said Mufasa. "All around you, as far as the eye can see, lies our kingdom. One day you will rule over it all."

Simba's eyes widened. "Do you think I'll be a good king, Father?" he asked.

Mufasa looked at his son. "You will if you remember that everything around us exists in a delicate balance – a great Circle of Life. You must take your place as king in that Circle and help to keep the balance."

Simba looked out towards the horizon. "What's that dark place over there?" he asked.

"It lies beyond our borders," said Mufasa. "You must never go there."

Just then Zazu arrived with news that some hyenas had been spotted on the Pride Lands. Looking worried, Mufasa ordered Zazu to take Simba home while he went to investigate.

Back at Pride Rock, Simba found his uncle snoozing in the shade.

"Guess what, Uncle Scar," cried Simba. "My father just showed me the whole kingdom – and one day I'll rule it all!"

Scar thought for a minute. Then he said slyly, "Did he show you the land beyond the northern border?"

"Well, no," admitted Simba. "He said I can't go there."

"Quite right," said Scar. "An elephant graveyard is *much* too dangerous for a young prince. Only the *bravest* of lions would go there!"

An elephant graveyard! It sounded exciting. Simba raced off at once to tell Nala, his best friend.

The two young cubs went out playing together. They scampered onto the plain, talking and giggling. Simba told Nala his exciting news about the elephant graveyard. As they raced ahead towards the forbidden place, they soon managed to lose Zazu, who had been sent to keep an eye on them.

The elephant graveyard lay shrouded in mist giving it an eerie atmosphere.

Simba tried hard to be brave. "Come on, Nala," he urged, heading towards a huge elephant skull. "I think something's in there."

At that moment, Zazu fluttered down beside them. He was *very* angry. "You must leave here *immediately*," he squawked. "We are all in great danger."

Suddenly three drooling hyenas emerged from the elephant skull.

Scar had ordered the hyenas to lay in wait in the graveyard to trap and kill the cubs.

Shenzi, a female hyena, circled Zazu. "You work for Mufasa," she said.

A second hyena, Banzai, approached Simba. "So you must be…" he began.

"The future King," said Simba, trying to sound as brave as possible.

"Do you know what we do with kings who step out of their kingdoms?" Shenzi asked Simba. "We have them for – dinner!"

Terrified, Simba and Nala fled and took refuge in a gigantic rib cage. Simba felt his heart beating wildly. He took a deep breath and tried to roar. But all he could produce was a squeaky rumble.

Ed, the third hyena laughed hysterically. Shenzi began to tease Simba. "Do it again, kitty, kitty."

Simba took another deep breath.

"ROAAARRR!"

The three hyenas spun round. They looked straight into the eyes of King Mufasa. He roared again, and Shenzi, Banzai and Ed fled howling into the mist.

Later, when they were alone, Mufasa told Simba how disappointed he was. "You disobeyed me," he said.

Simba hung his head in shame. "I was just trying to be brave like you," he mumbled. Simba knew he'd let his father down.

"I'm only brave when I have to be," replied Mufasa, gently.

"But you're not scared of *anything*," said Simba.

"I was scared today," said his father. "I thought I might lose you. Just remember, being brave doesn't mean you go looking for trouble."

The sun was setting. Soon a full moon appeared, and stars twinkled in the blackening sky.

"We'll always be together, won't we, Father?" asked Simba.

Mufasa stopped. "Look up at the sky," he said.

Simba gazed upwards.

"The great kings of the past look down at us from the stars. Whenever you feel alone just remember they'll always be there to guide you – and so will I."

Simba nodded. "I'll remember," he promised.

The next morning Simba followed Scar down to the bottom of a deep, wide gorge.

"Wait here," Scar told Simba. "Your father has a marvellous surprise for you." He turned to leave. "Now I'll go and tell him you're ready." Scar sauntered away, leaving his nephew all alone.

The hyenas were waiting at the entrance to the gorge. When Scar gave the signal they ran towards a herd of wildebeest forcing them to stampede in Simba's direction. The terrified cub clawed his way up onto the branch of a fallen tree.

Scar's plan was working perfectly. He ran to his brother's side. "Mufasa!" he called. "Quick! There's a stampede. Simba's trapped!"

Mufasa leapt into the gorge, grabbed Simba in his mouth and carried him to safety. However as he was climbing out of the gorge, Mufasa was knocked backwards by the galloping wildebeest.

Injured and in pain, he struggled to pull himself onto an overhanging rock. Slowly he looked up to see Scar leaning over him. "Help me," pleaded Mufasa.

Scar dug his claws into his brother's paws. "Long live the King," he snarled, pushing Mufasa back down into the path of the stampeding wildebeest.

When the dust finally settled, Scar found Simba sobbing over the body of his dead father.

"This is all *your* fault," Scar lied to Simba. "If it weren't for you, he'd still be alive. You must leave the Pride and *never* return."

Heartbroken, Simba fled. He staggered on until eventually, hot and exhausted, he collapsed in the desert. Hungry vultures began to circle overhead.

Meanwhile Scar had returned to Pride Rock and proclaimed himself as the new King. He told Sarabi that both Mufasa and Simba were dead.

But Simba was still alive! When he finally opened his eyes, Simba found a skinny meerkat and a fat warthog gazing down at him.

"My name is Timon," said the meerkat, "and this is Pumbaa."

"I have to go," said Simba, rising shakily to his feet.

"Where to?" asked Timon.

"I don't know," sighed Simba miserably. "I can't go back home, I've done something terrible."

"Then put your past behind you," said Timon, "and stay with us in the jungle. Take our advice – *hakuna matata* – no worries!"

Simba thought for a moment. He had nowhere else to go. "All right," he agreed.

"Good!" exclaimed Timon. "Now you must be hungry. Try this!"

Simba looked at the fat grub squirming in Timon's paw. It looked disgusting, but he was very hungry so he tried it. It tasted surprisingly good. Perhaps life in the jungle wouldn't be too bad after all!

The years passed by and Simba grew into a handsome young lion.

Although he loved his new friends, Simba was not really happy. He felt that something was missing from his carefree life.

Often, on starry nights, he would gaze up at the sky and remember his father's promise – *The stars will always be there to guide you* – *and so will I.*

One starry night Simba lay thinking. He was imagining what his father would think of him now. He sighed so deeply that his breath scattered a wispy puff of milkweed into the air.

A sudden wind sprang up and carried the milkweed far away into the waiting, outstretched hand of Rafiki, the old, mystic baboon who had blessed Simba as a cub.

Rafiki examined the seeds and hobbled into his cave and studied a picture on the wall that he had once painted. It was of a lion cub.

Rafiki broke open a gourd and smeared the sticky liquid around the cub's head. The picture magically changed into the image of a fully-grown lion, complete with a golden mane.

Rafiki smiled. "It's time," he whispered, and prepared to leave for the jungle.

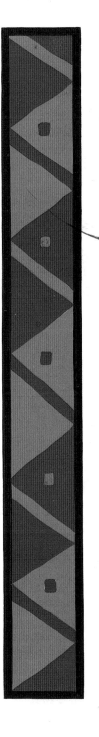

The next day Timon and Pumbaa were out hunting for bugs when Simba heard them cry and shout for help. He rushed to their aid and rescued them from a hungry lioness. As the lioness wrestled him to the ground, Simba looked at her closely and suddenly recognised who she was.

"Nala," he cried happily.

The two lions were delighted to see each other again. Simba introduced Nala to his friends then took her on a tour of his jungle home.

"It's just like paradise here," said Nala, "but Simba, you must return home. Things are terrible there. The plain is parched and barren since Scar took over the Pride and he lets the hyenas do whatever they want."

"I can't go back," said Simba. "I lead a different life now. *Hakuna matata* – no worries."

"Forget this *hakuna matata* nonsense, Simba," replied Nala. "Accept your responsibilities – you are the rightful King."

"I'm not fit to be king," said Simba quietly.

"You're hiding from the future," said Nala. "What would your father think?"

"My father is dead," said Simba sadly, and he turned and walked away.

That night Simba lay by a stream thinking about what Nala had said. Suddenly Simba heard a noise. Looking up he saw a wizened, old baboon – Rafiki.

Rafiki led Simba to a small pool. Above his head the clouds parted and Mufasa's image filled the sky.

"Simba, remember who you are," said the voice of Mufasa. "You are my son, and the one true King. You must take your place in the Circle of Life."

As Mufasa's image began to fade, Simba knew at once what he had to do – he must return to the Pride Lands.

*   *   *

At Pride Rock, the hyenas complained to Scar that they were hungry.

"It's the lionesses' job to hunt for food," snapped Scar. "Sarabi, where is your hunting party?"

"There is nothing left to hunt," said Sarabi. "We must all leave Pride Rock, or we will die of hunger."

"We're not going anywhere!" roared Scar. "I am the King, and I make the rules."

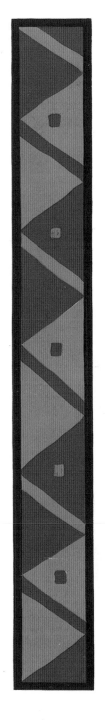

Suddenly a mighty roar filled the air. Scar turned round to see Simba.

"I've come back to take my place as the true King," said Simba.

Scar signalled to the pack of hyenas. Instantly they swarmed towards Simba. Caught off balance, Simba was pushed backwards, and he slipped over the cliff's edge. He struggled to cling to the crumbling rock.

"You look just the way your father did before I killed him," sneered Scar.

Scar's words filled Simba with new strength. He leapt up and knocked Scar aside.

Scar called to the hyenas to save him, but Nala and the lionesses drove them back.

A sudden flash of lightning ignited the dry grass around Pride Rock. As the fire blazed on all sides, Simba lunged at Scar, knocking him over the steep edge of the cliff to his death below.

"Welcome home," said Nala, as she smiled and nuzzled Simba. "Your mother is waiting to greet the new King."

As the whole Pride celebrated Simba's victory, the rain began to fall, putting out the flames and soaking the black, smoky ground. Within minutes, sheets of water drenched the plains, and gurgling streams snaked across the land once again.

With the arrival of the rain the Pride Lands came back to life. Green shoots sprang up from the fire blackened earth and the herds returned once more to graze on the plains.

*　　*　　*

Many months later birds and animals journeyed to Pride Rock once again to welcome another new prince into the world.

King Simba and Queen Nala watched proudly as Rafiki lifted *their* son high above the crowd.

Below Pride Rock the excited animals cheered and cried, "Welcome! Welcome to the new Prince!"

The Circle of Life was beginning again.

That night, after the crowd had gone, Simba stood alone at the top of Pride Rock, watching the sun set beyond the western hills.

"Everything's all right now, Father," Simba whispered, looking up at the star-filled sky. "You see, I remembered."

And one by one the stars seemed to twinkle in reply.